Bill Martin Jr & Michael Sampson

SWISH!

Illustrated by
Michael Chesworth

Henry Holt and Company · New York

To Lanelle and Leslie
—M.S.

Henry Holt and Company, Inc.
Publishers since 1866
115 West 18th Street
New York, New York 10011

Published in Canada by Fitzhenry & Whiteside Ltd.,
195 Allstate Parkway, Markham, Ontario L3R 4T8.

Library of Congress Cataloging-in-Publication Data
Martin, Bill. Swish! / Bill Martin Jr & Michael Sampson; illustrated by
Michael Chesworth.
Summary: Two girls' teams, the Cardinals and the Blue Jays, play a
close and intense game of basketball.
[1. Basketball—Fiction.] I. Sampson, Michael. II. Chesworth, Michael,
ill. III. Title. PZ7. M3643Sw 1997 [E]—dc20 96-44216

ISBN 0-8050-4498-1
First Edition—1997
Printed in the United States of America on acid-free paper.∞
10 9 8 7 6 5 4 3 2

Cardinals, Blue Jays...
what a game!

The winner goes
to the hall of fame.

Less than a minute left to play,
Blue Jays have the Cards at bay.

Referee hands the ball to Lynn,
Blue Jay pass comes bouncing in.

Dribble...

dribble...

dribble...

Janet passes off to Kim,

outside shot goes off the rim.

Katie leaping
from the ground,
hustles for a high rebound.

Then down the court Katie bounds,

Dribble...

dribble...

dribble...

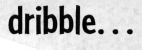

Jumping high into the sky,
she shoots. . .

Cardinal basket!

44 to 44,
only 16 seconds more.

Blue Jays rushing,
gotta score.

Slowing now
to a coast,
Marie breaks free,
to the post.

Inside move, what a dare,
jump shot flying through the air. . .

Blue Jay basket!

Teams gather around the bench,
sweaty towels wiping brows.
Gotta win, the coach shows how.

One last play, and no more,
the crowd lets out a mighty roar.

Teams clasp hands and make their vows. . .
scoreboard makes a blaring sound.

Cardinals pass to the floor,

Dribble. . .

dribble. . .

dribble. . .

Like a flash,

in comes Jill,

driving hard,

tries to steal!

But Katie comes out with the ball!
The crowd goes wild!

Dribble. . .

dribble. . .

Only 3 seconds more,
pass it now, we gotta score!

Allie's open on the side.
Fake it low, but toss it high. . .

Dribble. . .

Allie pivots on a dime,

throws to Cindi at the 3-point line.

Up she goes. . .
the world stands still.

Basketball spins,
arcing high. . .

Falling now,
from the sky. . .

whirling, swirling. . .

Buzzer blares, game's at end. . .
zero seconds,

Cardinals WIN!